DOLPHIN

FAST

ARMADILLO

SLOW

FOX

FAST

TIGER

FAST

KOALA

SLOW

OSTRICH

FAST

TORTOISE

SLOW

HEDGEHOG

SLOW

Snail Boy is dedicated to King Berlew —
my honourable lawyer, great friend
and protector of Snail Boy

First published 2003 by Walker Books Ltd
87 Vauxhall Walk, London SE11 5HJ

2 4 6 8 10 9 7 5 3 1

© 2003 Leslie McGuirk

This book has been typeset in Gararond

Printed in Hong Kong

British Library Cataloguing in Publication Data:
a catalogue record for this book
is available from the British Library

ISBN 0-7445-8002-1

Snail Boy

LESLIE McGUIRK

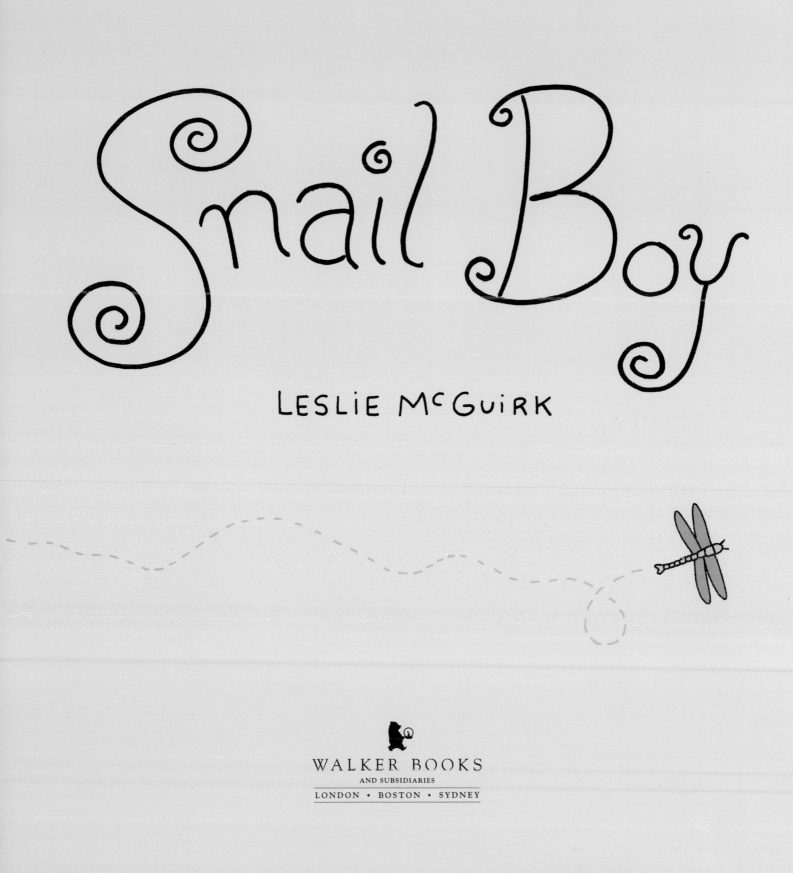

WALKER BOOKS
AND SUBSIDIARIES
LONDON • BOSTON • SYDNEY

This is Snail.

He is a Gigantic Exotic Gastropod in full bloom.

He is as big as this pony.

Snail is extremely rare, so he hides most of the day.

He's afraid the wrong kind of person, like a Snail Hunter, will catch him.

At night he sleeps in his secret hiding-place
and has bad dreams.

One morning, Snail woke up and had a life-saving idea.

But he needed to find just the right owner.

He began his search at the local park. He climbed a giant tree and looked down at his prospects.

There was one boy — a boy with a red cap — who was playing by himself.

"I'll ask him," said Snail, "because he's alone, like me."

Snail crawled back down to the ground.
He waited inside his shell.

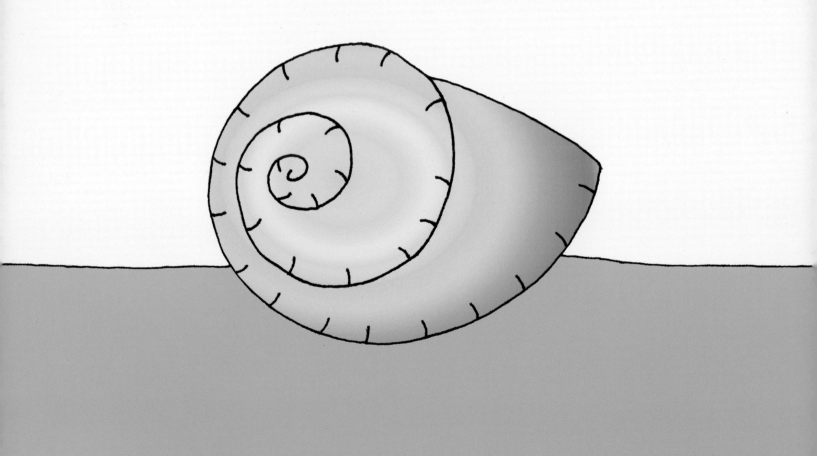

When the boy ran past, Snail popped out and said,
"Do you have time…"

But before he could finish the boy screamed.

"You scared me," said the boy. "You're as big as a pony!"

"Yes," said Snail, "but I'm better-looking and much more interesting. Do you have time to look after a pet like me?"

The boy laughed. "You must be joking! You're just a big slowcoach. If you were a cheetah, I might be interested."

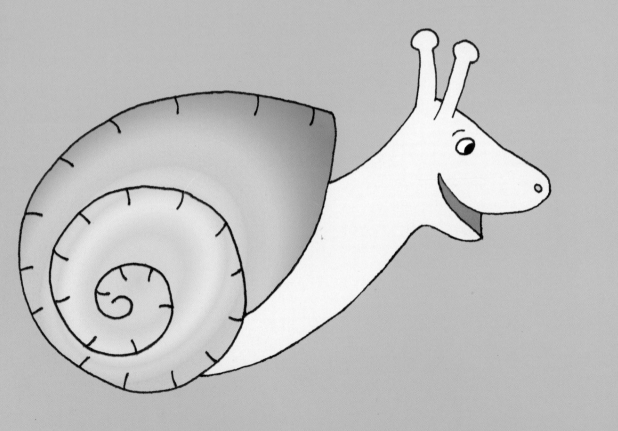

"A cheetah!" scoffed Snail.
"Fast pets just leave you in the dust.
   I wouldn't leave you in the dust or anywhere else!
   Plus you wouldn't need to brush me."

"Can you do tricks?" asked the boy.

"Of course! Watch this," said Snail.

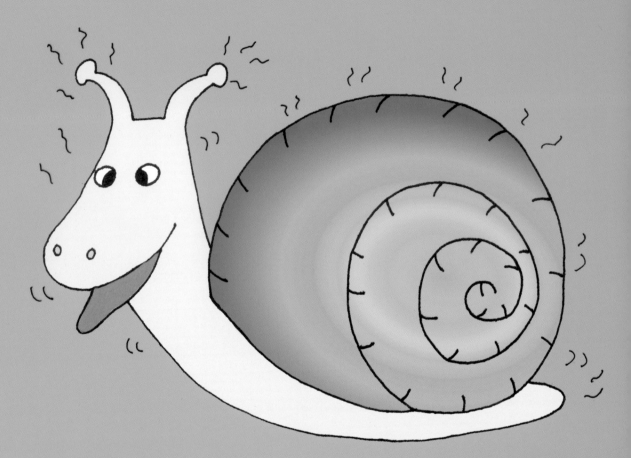

Snail shook his whole body.

"What was that?" asked the boy.

"SHAKE!" answered Snail with pride.
The boy laughed.

"Now watch this," said Snail, and he showed
the boy the rest of his tricks.

ROLL OVER!   PLAY DEAD!

"I think talking is my best trick of all,
though, don't you?" Snail asked.

"Definitely," said the boy. "It's a shame I'm
still not really looking for a pet."

"Oh well," said Snail. "I was just imagining how good you would look, up on my back."

"You mean I could ride you?" asked the boy.

"Normally only licensed snail operators can ride me, but if you were my owner..."

"All right!" said the boy. "I'll be your owner!"

"Great!" said Snail. "Hop on. You are now my official Snail Boy."

And slowly, slowly they made their way to the pet shop.

Together they chose a collar, two dishes, snail food and some toys.

When they passed the hamster display,
the boy told them, "The snail's mine!"

As they left the shop, it started to rain.

"We're going to get wet," announced Snail Boy.

845,42/JJF

"Let's go inside my shell," said Snail.

Snail squeezed in first.

The boy followed.

"It's nice and cozy in here and really pink," said the boy.

"I'm glad you like it," said Snail.

"This can be our own private club!" said the boy.
Snail thought that was an excellent idea.

They talked for a long time — about what
they wanted to be when they grew up and
what they were going to have for dinner.
Then the rain stopped falling and they
climbed out.

"That was fun," said Snail Boy.
"I'm really lucky you're my pet."

Snail replied with a word that sounded like a backwards hiccup. It meant "thank you" in Snailese.

And from that day on Snail and Snail Boy were best friends.

WORM

SLOW

SLOTH

MANATEE

SLOW

CHEETAH

FAST

PANDA

SLOW

FISH

FAST

HUMMINGBIRD

FAST